Youri Vinitchouk • Kost Lav

Le plus brave des petits COCHONS

BAYARD JEUNESSE

Voici la drôle d'histoire d'un petit cochon qui rêvait de voyager.
Il en rêvait même tellement que…

Un jour, le petit cochon arrive chez le roi.
Quand le roi l'aperçoit, il se met à crier :
– D'où sort-il, celui-là ?
Un petit cochon chez moi ?
Qu'on le mette dehors, et plus vite que ça !
C'était un roi qui aimait bien dire :
– Et plus vite que ça !

Les gardes du roi se jettent sur le petit cochon.
Mais pas moyen de l'attraper !
Le petit cochon court si vite
qu'il arrive toujours à s'échapper.
Le roi est très en colère :
– Saleté de petit cochon !
Tirez-lui dessus !
Et plus vite que ça !

Alors les ministres pointent leurs grands fusils
et leurs gros pistolets, et ils tirent tous
en même temps. PAN PAN ! PAN PAN !
Mais le petit cochon évite toutes les balles
et il s'en sort sans une égratignure !
Puis il s'en va, en remuant gaiement
sa petite queue en tire-bouchon.

Le petit cochon court, il court dans la forêt.
Mais voilà qu'il tombe nez à nez
avec une bande de terribles brigands.
Les brigands menacent le petit cochon :
– Donne-nous ton argent, petit cochon !
Et plus vite que ça !
Eux aussi, ils aimaient bien dire :
– Et plus vite que ça !

Mais le petit cochon se jette bravement
dans leurs jambes, et alors quelle pagaille !
ZIP ZIP ! Les couteaux sifflent au-dessus de sa tête.
BANG BANG ! Les pistolets claquent.
Et quand la bataille est terminée,
le petit cochon découvre
tous les brigands assommés à ses pieds.
– Bien fait pour vous ! dit-il.

Le petit cochon continue sa route
et il arrive au bord de la mer.
Là, il voit des marins.
–Waouh ! s'écrie le petit cochon.
J'aimerais tellement devenir un marin, moi aussi !
Les marins se moquent de lui :
–Hein ? Tu nous as bien regardés ?
Il est complètement fou, celui-là !
On n'est pas des marins, on est des pirates,
voilà ce qu'on est !
Alors le petit cochon s'exclame :
–Merveilleux ! Tout simplement merveilleux !
Toute ma vie, j'ai rêvé d'être un capitaine de pirates !
Les pirates rient à qui mieux mieux.
Mais le petit cochon insiste tellement
qu'ils l'emmènent sur leur bateau.

Et les pirates ne le regrettent pas !
Très vite, le petit cochon leur montre comme il est brave.

Il est le premier à se lancer à l'abordage et il met tant de cœur à se battre que bientôt les pirates n'ont plus qu'à se reposer.

Le petit cochon dirige le bateau avec tellement de succès
qu'il est choisi pour devenir chef des pirates !
Les pirates deviennent incroyablement riches !
Le petit cochon, lui, devient incroyablement célèbre,
si bien que tout le monde, dans tous les ports,
l'accueille et l'admire... énormément !

Même le roi de France
décide de lui donner sa fille en mariage !
Quand la princesse apprend ça, elle se sent mal :
– Mama mia ! Moi ? Épouser un petit cochon ?
Oh non !
Alors le roi déclare :
– Mais ce ne sera plus un petit cochon !
Je vais le nommer grand amiral
de tous les bateaux du roi !
Espérons seulement qu'il acceptera…

Sans plus attendre,
le roi envoie ses ambassadeurs.
Le petit cochon les écoute avec attention.
–Bien, dit-il, ça marche ! Je veux bien être amiral !
Et pour la princesse, j'accepte aussi
mais à une condition : elle doit apprendre
à préparer les boulettes aux pommes de terre,
c'est ce que je préfère !

Quand la princesse a appris à cuisiner
les boulettes de pommes de terre,
le petit cochon l'épouse.
Il est si beau, avec son épée au côté
et son chapeau à plume,
que la princesse se met à l'aimer… follement !

Puis les mariés partent en voyage :
ils veulent découvrir le monde.
Ils traversent tous les pays, et sur leur chemin
tout le monde se précipite pour admirer
le petit cochon, le plus brave des petits cochons,
le vainqueur des brigands,
la terreur des mers et des océans,
le grand amiral des bateaux du roi !
Tout le monde l'applaudit :
– Qu'il est beau ! Qu'il est grand !
Vive notre héros !

Mais un jour, le petit cochon arrive dans son pays.
Là, les gens ne se laissent pas avoir :
ils ne voient pas le grand amiral des bateaux du roi,
ils voient un petit cochon, un point c'est tout.

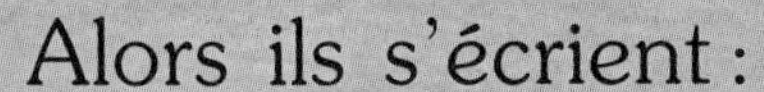

Alors ils s'écrient :
– Oh, oh, regardez-moi ça ! Un cochon dans un carrosse !
Avec une princesse, en plus !
Quand le petit cochon entend ça,
il brandit son épée et il crie à son tour :
– Ignorants, bons à rien, cochons vous-mêmes !
Il trépigne, il grogne, il bouge tellement…

…que ça finit par le réveiller !
Autour de lui, des poules caquettent :
– Hé, petit cochon, qu'est-ce qui te prend ?
Pourquoi tu fais tout ce boucan ?
Alors le petit cochon bâille :
– Oh, c'est rien, ça va ! Je reviens de voyage…

C'était la drôle d'histoire d'un petit cochon
qui voyageait beaucoup… en rêve !

Dans la collection

les belles HISTOIRES

Les mots de Zaza
Jacqueline Cohen • Bernadette Després

L'ogre qui avait peur des enfants
Marie-Hélène Delval • Pierre Denieuil

Ma maman a besoin de moi
Mildred Pitts Walter • Claude et Denise Millet

Le grand voyage de Nils Holgersson
d'après l'œuvre originale de Selma Lagerlöf
Catherine de Lasa • Carme Solé Vendrell

L'ours qui voulait qu'on l'aime
Claire Clément • Carme Solé Vendrell

La famille Cochon déménage
Marie-Agnès Gaudrat • Colette Camil

Le petit ogre veut aller à l'école
Marie-Agnès Gaudrat • David Parkins

La sorcière qui rapetissait les enfants
Véronique Caylou • David Parkins

Le loup vert
René Gouichoux • Éric Gasté

Le pré sans fleurs ni couleurs
Laurence Gillot • Antoon Krings

Le chant du sorcier
Carl Norac • Claude Cachin

La soupe à la grimace
Hélène Leroy • Éric Gasté

Le secret de la petite souris
Alain Chiche • Anne Wilsdorf

Le petit monsieur tout seul
Barbro Lindgren • Ulises Wensell

Retrouvez aussi tous les mois le magazine *Les Belles Histoires*,
avec une grande histoire inédite, les aventures de Zouk, la petite sorcière,
les rencontres merveilleuses des Trois Cochons Petits et les héros de la mythologie.

ISBN 13 : 978-2-7470-2531-7

Texte de Youri Vinitchouk, illustrations de Kost Lavro
Dépôt légal : avril 2008
Impression en France par Pollina s.a., 85400 Luçon - L45504B
Loi 49-956 du 16 juillet 1949
sur les publications destinées à la jeunesse

Publications International, Ltd.
Favorite Brand Name Recipes at www.fbnr.com

Louis Weber, CEO
Publications International, Ltd.
7373 North Cicero Avenue
Lincolnwood, IL 60712

Pictured on the front cover: Ranch Tuna Stuffed Tomato *(page 68).*
Pictured on the back cover *(clockwise from top):* Chicken Caesar Tetrazzini *(page 52)*, Red Pepper Dip *(page 22)* and Hidden Valley® Wraps *(page 88).*

ISBN-13: 978-1-4127-2279-7
ISBN-10: 1-4127-2279-9

Manufactured in China.

8 7 6 5 4 3 2 1

Microwave Cooking: Microwave ovens vary in wattage. Use the cooking times as guidelines and check for doneness before adding more time.

CONTENTS

The Best Tasting Solution... Every Time

Despite the many rewards today's active lifestyles offer, trying to balance career, home life and still find time to relax with a good book or workout at the gym can also make you feel like a juggler with one too many balls in the air.

And if you are a working parent, you often find yourself juggling the choices that your children or spouse make as well—from finding time to attend your kid's soccer game to preparing a delicious, well-balanced meal that everyone in your family will enjoy. That's why we at Hidden Valley® created the Original Ranch® recipes featured in this cookbook to give you delicious solutions. Whether you favor the bolder tastes of Pork Tenderloin with Red Pepper Sauce and Ranch Baked Quesadillas, or the milder creamy texture of Original Ranch® Mashed Potatoes, you can be sure with these Ranch favorites there will be plenty of good taste to go around. And on those occasions when you entertain larger groups, you may want to try our Roasted Red Pepper Spread or Ranch Drummettes and Potato Skins, which offer a colorful and tangy alternative to more traditional hors d'oeuvres.

At Hidden Valley®, we know you face enough tough decisions every day. Hopefully, with the help of these new recipes, deciding what to eat won't be one of them.

This book is the result of our commitment to showcase our specialties in a new collection of Hidden Valley® recipes. Because some basic foods blend so well with the Hidden Valley® flavor profile, those foods are used in many different dishes. To assist you with preparing these recipes, our food pros offer a few preparation tips:

- *Toss salads in Glad® Zipper Storage Bags. This eliminates the mess and damage to salad ingredients.*
- *Use a salad spinner for drying greens or buy prewashed greens.*
- *Substitute crushed salad croutons for toasted or buttered bread crumbs.*
- *Squeeze all the liquid from cooked spinach before adding to a recipe. This prevents the recipe from becoming watery and green in color.*
- *Freeze nuts for storing. Frozen nuts maintain a clean appearance when chopped in the food processor.*
- *Plan ahead. Cook extra rice and pasta for another meal. Store in Glad® Zipper Storage Bags and reheat in the microwave oven.*
- *Thaw frozen food in the refrigerator—not on the counter.*
- *Provide children with their own table of snacks. During cold and flu season, it might be wise to provide individual snack plates along with serving spoons for the dip.*
- *Recycle leftovers into new meals. Tonight's leftover dip is a topper for tomorrow's baked potato. Or, that wilted green salad becomes a vegetable soup base when puréed in the food processor.*

Lastly, I encourage you to be daring in the kitchen. Today is history and tomorrow is a mystery. Create that culinary mystery with a little Hidden Valley® magic.

Mary M. BoMarc, CFCS
Hidden Valley Kitchens

APPEALING APPETIZERS

Original Ranch® Spinach Dip

MAKES 2½ CUPS

1 container (16 ounces) sour cream (2 cups)
1 box (10 ounces) frozen chopped spinach, thawed and squeezed dry
1 can (8 ounces) water chestnuts, rinsed, drained and chopped
1 packet (1 ounce) Hidden Valley® Original Ranch® Seasoning & Salad Dressing Mix
1 loaf round French bread
Fresh vegetables, for dipping

Stir together sour cream, spinach, water chestnuts and seasoning & salad dressing mix. Chill 30 minutes. Just before serving, cut top off bread and remove center, reserving firm bread pieces. Fill bread bowl with dip. Cut reserved bread into cubes. Serve dip with bread and vegetables.

Original Ranch® Snack Mix

MAKES 10 CUPS

- 8 cups Kellogg's® Crispix® cereal
- 2½ cups small pretzels
- 2½ cups bite-size Cheddar cheese crackers
- 3 tablespoons vegetable oil
- 1 packet (1 ounce) Hidden Valley® Original Ranch® Seasoning & Salad Dressing Mix

Combine cereal, pretzels and crackers in a gallon-size Glad® Zipper Storage Bag. Pour oil over mixture. Seal bag and toss to coat. Add seasoning & salad dressing mix; seal bag and toss again until coated.

Top to bottom:
Original Ranch® Snack Mix and
Original Ranch® Oyster Crackers (page 14)

Hidden Valley® Pinwheels

MAKES 3 DOZEN APPETIZERS

- 2 packages (8 ounces *each*) cream cheese, softened
- 1 packet (1 ounce) Hidden Valley® Original Ranch® Seasoning & Salad Dressing Mix
- 2 green onions, minced
- 4 (12-inch) flour tortillas
- 1 jar (4 ounces) diced pimientos, rinsed and drained
- 1 can (4 ounces) diced green chiles, rinsed and drained
- 1 can (2¼ ounces) sliced ripe olives, rinsed and drained

Mix cream cheese, seasoning & salad dressing mix and onions until blended. Spread on tortillas. Blot dry pimientos, chiles and olives on paper towels. Sprinkle equal amounts of pimientos, chiles and olives over cream cheese mixture. Roll tortillas tightly in Glad® Cling Wrap. Chill at least 2 hours. Cut rolls into 1-inch pieces; discarding ends. Serve with spirals facing up.

Hidden Valley® Cheese Fingers

MAKES ABOUT 48 FINGERS

- 2 small loaves (8 ounces *each*) French bread, cut in half lengthwise
- 1 package (8 ounces) cream cheese, softened
- 1 packet (1 ounce) Hidden Valley® Original Ranch® Seasoning & Salad Dressing Mix
- 4 cups assorted toppings, such as chopped onions, bell peppers and shredded cheese

Slice bread crosswise into 1-inch fingers, leaving fingers attached to crust. Mix together cream cheese and seasoning & salad dressing mix. Spread on cut sides of bread. Sprinkle on desired toppings. Broil about 3 minutes or until brown and bubbly.

Roasted Red Pepper Spread

Makes 2 cups

1 cup roasted red peppers, rinsed and drained
1 package (8 ounces) cream cheese, softened
1 packet (1 ounce) Hidden Valley® Original Ranch® Seasoning & Salad Dressing Mix
Baguette slices and sliced ripe olives (optional)

Blot dry red peppers. In a food processor fitted with a metal blade, combine peppers, cream cheese and seasoning & salad dressing mix; process until smooth. Spread on baguette slices and garnish with olives, if desired.

Original Ranch® Oyster Crackers

Makes 8 cups

1 box (16 ounces) oyster crackers
¼ cup vegetable oil
1 packet (1 ounce) Hidden Valley® Original Ranch® Seasoning & Salad Dressing Mix

Place crackers in a gallon-size Glad® Zipper Storage Bag. Pour oil over crackers; seal bag and toss to coat. Add seasoning & salad dressing mix; seal bag and toss again until coated. Bake on ungreased baking sheet at 250°F. for 15 to 20 minutes or until crackers are golden brown.

Roasted Red Pepper Spread

Ranch Drummettes

Makes 6 to 8 servings (or 24 drummettes)

- ½ cup butter or margarine
- ¼ cup hot pepper sauce
- 3 tablespoons vinegar
- 24 chicken wing drummettes
- 1 packet (1 ounce) Hidden Valley® Original Ranch® Seasoning & Salad Dressing Mix
- ½ teaspoon paprika
- Additional prepared Hidden Valley® Original Ranch® Seasoning & Salad Dressing Mix
- Celery sticks (optional)

Melt butter and whisk together with pepper sauce and vinegar in a small bowl. Dip drummettes in butter mixture; arrange in a single layer in a large baking pan. Sprinkle with seasoning & salad dressing mix. Bake at 350°F. for 30 to 40 minutes or until juices run clear and chicken is browned. Sprinkle with paprika. Serve with additional prepared seasoning & salad dressing mix and celery sticks, if desired.

Top to bottom: Potato Skins (page 18) and Ranch Drummettes

Potato Skins

MAKES 8 TO 10 SERVINGS

- 4 baked potatoes, quartered
- ¼ cup sour cream
- 1 packet (1 ounce) Hidden Valley® Original Ranch® Seasoning & Salad Dressing Mix
- 1 cup (4 ounces) shredded Cheddar cheese
- Sliced green onions and/or bacon pieces* (optional)

**Crisp-cooked, crumbled bacon may be used.*

Scoop potato out of skins; combine potatoes with sour cream and seasoning & salad dressing mix. Fill skins with mixture. Sprinkle with cheese. Bake at 375°F. for 12 to 15 minutes or until cheese is melted. Garnish with green onions and/or bacon bits, if desired.

Artichoke and Crabmeat Party Dip

MAKES 3½ CUPS

- 1 container (16 ounces) sour cream (2 cups)
- 1 packet (1 ounce) Hidden Valley® Original Ranch® Dips Mix
- 1 can (14 ounces) artichoke hearts, rinsed, drained and chopped
- ¾ cup cooked crabmeat, rinsed and drained
- 2 tablespoons chopped red or green bell pepper
- French bread slices, crackers or fresh vegetables, for dipping

Combine sour cream and dips mix. Stir in artichoke hearts, crabmeat and bell pepper. Chill 30 minutes. Serve with French bread, crackers or fresh vegetables.

Hidden Valley® Bacon-Cheddar Ranch Dip

MAKES ABOUT 3 CUPS

1 container (16 ounces) sour cream (2 cups)
1 packet (1 ounce) Hidden Valley® Original Ranch® Dips Mix
1 cup (4 ounces) shredded Cheddar cheese
¼ cup crisp-cooked, crumbled bacon*
Potato chips or corn chips, for dipping

**Bacon pieces may be used.*

Combine sour cream and dips mix. Stir in cheese and bacon. Chill at least 1 hour. Serve with chips.

Ranch Artichoke Spread

MAKES 1½ CUPS

1 can (14 ounces) artichoke hearts, rinsed and drained
¾ cup Hidden Valley® Original Ranch® Dressing
¼ cup sour cream
¼ cup grated Parmesan cheese
Crackers or French bread slices

Coarsely chop artichokes and combine with dressing, sour cream and Parmesan cheese. Chill 30 minutes. Spread on crackers or bread slices to serve.

Hidden Valley® Bacon-Cheddar Ranch Dip

Hidden Valley® Salsa Ranch Dip

MAKES 2½ CUPS

1 container (16 ounces) sour cream (2 cups)
1 packet (1 ounce) Hidden Valley® Original Ranch® Dips Mix
½ cup thick and chunky salsa
Chopped tomatoes and diced green chiles (optional)
Tortilla chips, for dipping

Combine sour cream and dips mix. Stir in salsa. Add tomatoes and chiles, if desired. Chill 1 hour. Serve with tortilla chips.

Red Pepper Dip

MAKES 2 CUPS

6 ounces roasted red peppers, rinsed and drained
1 cup Hidden Valley® Original Ranch® Dressing
1 package (8 ounces) cream cheese, softened
Hot cooked chicken nuggets

In a food processor fitted with a metal blade, purée peppers. Add dressing and cream cheese; process until smooth. Chill 30 minutes. Serve with chicken nuggets.

Hidden Valley® Salsa Ranch Dip

7-Layer Sombrero Dip

MAKES 8 TO 10 SERVINGS

1 can (16 ounces) refried beans
1 container (8 ounces) sour cream (1 cup)
1 packet (1 ounce) Hidden Valley® Original Ranch® Seasoning & Salad Dressing Mix
1 cup diced tomatoes
1 can (4 ounces) diced green chiles, rinsed and drained
1 can (2¼ ounces) sliced ripe olives, rinsed and drained
¾ cup (3 ounces) shredded Cheddar cheese
¾ cup (3 ounces) shredded Monterey Jack cheese
Chopped avocado (optional)
Tortilla chips, for dipping

Spread beans on a 10-inch serving platter. Blend sour cream and seasoning & salad dressing mix. Spread over beans. Layer tomatoes, chiles, olives, Cheddar cheese, Monterey Jack cheese and avocado, if desired. Serve with tortilla chips.

Maple Dijon Dip

Makes 1 cup

1 cup Hidden Valley® Original Ranch® Dressing
4 teaspoons pure maple syrup
1 teaspoon Dijon mustard
Hot cooked chicken nuggets (optional)

Stir together dressing, syrup and mustard in a small bowl. Chill 30 minutes. Serve with chicken nuggets, if desired.

Original Ranch® Meatballs

Makes 2 dozen

1 pound ground beef
1 packet (1 ounce) Hidden Valley® Original Ranch® Seasoning & Salad Dressing Mix
2 tablespoons butter or margarine
½ cup beef broth

Combine ground beef and seasoning & salad dressing mix. Shape into meatballs. Melt butter in a skillet; brown meatballs on all sides. Add broth; cover and simmer 10 to 15 minutes or until cooked through. Serve warm with toothpicks.

ENTICING ENTRÉES

Ranch Chicken Pizza

MAKES 8 SERVINGS

½ cup Hidden Valley® Original Ranch® Dressing
1 package (3 ounces) cream cheese, softened
2 tablespoons tomato paste
1 cup chopped cooked chicken
1 (12-inch) prebaked pizza crust
½ cup roasted red pepper strips, rinsed and drained
1 can (2¼ ounces) sliced ripe olives, drained
¼ cup chopped green onions
1 cup (4 ounces) shredded mozzarella cheese

Preheat oven to 450°F. Beat dressing, cream cheese and tomato paste until smooth. Stir in chicken; spread mixture on pizza crust. Arrange red peppers, olives and onions on pizza; sprinkle with mozzarella cheese. Bake at 450°F. for 15 minutes or until hot and bubbly.

Burrito Wraps

Makes 4 to 6 servings

- 2 cups shredded cooked chicken
- 1 container (8 ounces) sour cream (1 cup)
- ½ cup salsa
- 1 packet (1 ounce) Hidden Valley® Original Ranch® Seasoning & Salad Dressing Mix
- 4 to 6 (10-inch) flour tortillas, warmed
- Fillings, such as black beans, lettuce, cabbage, red pepper strips and cheese (optional)

Combine chicken, sour cream, salsa and seasoning & salad dressing mix in saucepan; heat thoroughly. Fill tortillas with chicken mixture and desired fillings. Roll up tortillas to enclose fillings.

Ultimate Ranch Cheese Burgers

Makes 4 servings

- 1 pound ground beef
- 1 cup (4 ounces) shredded Cheddar cheese
- 1 packet (1 ounce) Hidden Valley® Original Ranch® Seasoning & Salad Dressing Mix
- 4 hamburger buns

Combine beef, cheese and seasoning & salad dressing mix. Shape into 4 patties; cook thoroughly until no longer pink in the center. Toast buns before serving, if desired.

Ranch Clam Chowder

MAKES 4 TO 6 SERVINGS

- 3 cans (6½ ounces *each*) chopped clams
- 6 slices bacon, chopped*
- ¼ cup finely chopped onion
- ¼ cup all-purpose flour
- 2½ cups milk
- 1 packet (1 ounce) Hidden Valley® Original Ranch® Seasoning & Salad Dressing Mix
- 2 cups frozen cubed O'Brien potatoes
- 2 cups frozen corn kernels
- ⅛ teaspoon dried thyme (optional)

**Bacon pieces may be used.*

Drain clams, reserving juice (about 1⅓ cups); set aside. Cook bacon until crisp in a large pot or Dutch oven; remove with slotted spoon, reserving ¼ cup drippings.** Set aside bacon pieces. Heat bacon drippings over medium heat in same pot. Add onion; sauté 3 minutes. Sprinkle with flour; cook and stir 1 minute longer. Gradually whisk in reserved clam juice and milk, stirring until smooth. Whisk in seasoning & salad dressing mix until blended. Stir in potatoes, corn and thyme, if desired. Bring mixture just to a boil; reduce heat and simmer 10 minutes, stirring occasionally. Stir in clams; heat through. Sprinkle bacon on each serving.

***¼ cup butter may be used.*

Ranch Crispy Chicken

Makes 4 to 6 servings

- 1/4 cup unseasoned dry bread crumbs or cornflake crumbs
- 1 packet (1 ounce) Hidden Valley® Original Ranch® Seasoning & Salad Dressing Mix
- 6 bone-in chicken pieces

Combine bread crumbs and seasoning & salad dressing mix in a gallon-size Glad® Zipper Storage Bag. Add chicken pieces; seal bag. Shake to coat chicken. Bake chicken on ungreased baking pan at 375°F. for 50 minutes or until no longer pink in center and juices run clear.

Savory Baked Fish

Makes 6 servings

- 6 boneless fish fillets, such as scrod, flounder or other mild white fish (about 8 ounces *each*)
- 3/4 cup Hidden Valley® Original Ranch® Dressing
- Julienned vegetables, cooked (optional)

Arrange fish fillets in a large oiled baking pan. Spread each fillet with 2 tablespoons dressing. Bake at 375°F. for 10 to 20 minutes, depending on thickness of fish, or until fish flakes when tested with a fork. Finish under broiler to brown top. Serve on julienned vegetables, if desired.

Ranch Crispy Chicken

Pork Tenderloin with Red Pepper Sauce

MAKES 1¼ CUPS SAUCE

- 1 cup chopped onion
- ¼ cup olive oil
- 1 cup roasted red peppers, rinsed and drained
- ¾ cup sour cream
- 1 packet (1 ounce) Hidden Valley® Original Ranch® Seasoning & Salad Dressing Mix
- 2 pork tenderloins (about 1 pound each), cooked and sliced

Sauté onion in olive oil in a large skillet until soft and lightly browned. Stir in red peppers and heat through. Remove skillet from heat; stir in sour cream and seasoning & salad dressing mix. Transfer warm mixture to food processor and purée until smooth. Serve warm over sliced pork tenderloin.

SERVING SUGGESTION: This sauce is also good served over steak and chicken or used cold as a sandwich spread.

Pork Tenderloin with Red Pepper Sauce

Ranch Chicken with Cheese

Makes 4 servings

½ cup Hidden Valley® Original Ranch® Dressing
1 tablespoon all-purpose flour
4 boneless, skinless chicken breast halves (about 1 pound)
¼ cup (1 ounce) shredded sharp Cheddar cheese
¼ cup grated Parmesan cheese

Combine dressing and flour in a shallow bowl. Coat each chicken breast with dressing mixture. Place on ungreased baking pan. Combine Cheddar and Parmesan cheeses; sprinkle on chicken. Bake at 375°F. for 25 minutes or until chicken is no longer pink in center and juices run clear.

Original Ranch® Pork Chops

Makes 4 to 6 servings

1 packet (1 ounce) Hidden Valley® Original Ranch® Seasoning & Salad Dressing Mix
¼ teaspoon black pepper
6 pork chops (about ¾-inch thick)
Dash of paprika

Combine seasoning & salad dressing mix and pepper. Rub mixture on both sides of pork chops. Arrange pork chops in a single layer in a shallow baking pan. Sprinkle with paprika. Bake at 450°F. for 20 to 25 minutes or until cooked through.

Skillet Fajitas

MAKES 4 SERVINGS

- 1 packet (1 ounce) Hidden Valley® Original Ranch® Seasoning & Salad Dressing Mix
- 2 tablespoons olive oil
- 1 tablespoon water
- 1½ pounds beef flank steak, cut into thin strips
- 3 cups mixed bell peppers and onion strips
- 4 (10-inch) flour tortillas, warmed
- Fillings, such as guacamole, salsa and sour cream (optional)

Combine seasoning & salad dressing mix with oil and water. Sauté steak strips in dressing mixture in a large skillet. Add bell peppers and onions; cook until tender-crisp. Place mixture in tortillas. Add fillings, if desired. Roll up tortillas to enclose fillings.

Original Ranch® Ravioli

MAKES 3 TO 4 SERVINGS

½ cup roasted red peppers, rinsed and drained
1 package (9 ounces) refrigerated meat or chicken ravioli
1 cup Hidden Valley® Original Ranch® Dressing
¼ cup grated Parmesan cheese

Blot dry peppers; cut into thin strips. Cook ravioli according to package directions; drain and combine with pepper strips and dressing in a large nonstick skillet. Cook and stir over medium heat until mixture is hot. Garnish with cheese.

Original Ranch® Ravioli

Hidden Valley® Broiled Fish

MAKES 4 SERVINGS

- 1 packet (1 ounce) Hidden Valley® Original Ranch® Seasoning & Salad Dressing Mix
- ⅓ cup lemon juice
- 3 tablespoons olive oil
- 3 tablespoons dry white wine or water
- 1½ to 2 pounds mild white fish fillets, such as red snapper or sole

Combine seasoning & salad dressing mix, lemon juice, olive oil and wine in a shallow dish; mix well. Add fish and coat all sides with mixture. Cover and refrigerate for 15 to 30 minutes. Remove fish from marinade and place on broiler pan. Broil 9 to 12 minutes or until fish begins to flake when tested with a fork.

Hidden Valley® Broiled Fish

Lemon Chicken

MAKES 4 SERVINGS

1 packet (1 ounce) Hidden Valley® Original Ranch® Seasoning & Salad Dressing Mix
1 tablespoon cornstarch
4 boneless, skinless chicken breast halves
3 tablespoons butter or margarine
1 cup chicken broth
3 tablespoons lemon juice
1 tablespoon sugar
½ teaspoon lemon zest
¼ cup thinly sliced green onions
2 cups hot cooked rice (optional)
2 tablespoons finely chopped fresh parsley (optional)

Mix seasoning & salad dressing mix with cornstarch in a small bowl. Remove 2 tablespoons of mixture and lightly dust chicken breasts. Reserve remaining mixture for sauce. Melt butter in a large skillet over medium heat; lightly brown chicken on both sides. Remove pan from heat; remove chicken. Stir together chicken broth, lemon juice, sugar and lemon zest. Whisk into reserved cornstarch mixture. Add to skillet; cook and stir over low heat 1 to 2 minutes or until thickened. Return chicken to skillet. Cover and simmer gently on low heat for about 15 minutes or until chicken is no longer pink, adding onions during last 5 minutes. Serve with rice mixed with parley, if desired.

Pizza Blanco

MAKES 8 SERVINGS

½ cup grated Parmesan cheese
1 (12-inch) prebaked pizza crust
3 plum tomatoes, thinly sliced
½ cup Hidden Valley® Original Ranch® Dressing
½ cup roasted red pepper strips, rinsed and drained
1 can (2¼ ounces) sliced ripe olives, drained
¼ cup sliced green onions
1 cup (4 ounces) shredded mozzarella and Cheddar cheese blend

Preheat oven to 450°F. Sprinkle Parmesan cheese on pizza crust; cover with a single layer of tomato slices. Drizzle dressing over tomatoes. Arrange red pepper, olives and onions on pizza; sprinkle with cheese blend. Bake at 450°F. for 15 minutes or until cheese is melted and crust is hot.

Green Chile Chicken Enchiladas

Makes 4 servings

2 cups shredded cooked chicken
1½ cups (6 ounces) shredded Mexican cheese blend or Cheddar cheese, divided
½ cup Hidden Valley® Original Ranch® Dressing
¼ cup sour cream
2 tablespoons canned diced green chiles, rinsed and drained
4 (9 to 10-inch) flour tortillas, warmed

Mix together chicken, ¾ cup cheese, dressing, sour cream and green chiles in a medium bowl. Divide evenly down center of each tortilla. Roll up tortillas and place, seam side down, in a 9-inch baking dish. Top with remaining ¾ cup cheese. Bake at 350°F. for 20 minutes or until cheese is melted and lightly browned.

Note: Purchase rotisserie chicken at your favorite store to add great taste and save preparation time.

Green Chile Chicken Enchilada

Tuna Skillet Supper

MAKES 4 TO 6 SERVINGS

1 package (8 ounces) cream cheese, softened
1 cup milk
1 packet (1 ounce) Hidden Valley® Original Ranch® Seasoning & Salad Dressing Mix
8 ounces uncooked spiral egg noodles
2 cups frozen petite peas, thawed
2 cans (6 ounces *each*) tuna or shrimp, drained

In a food processor fitted with a metal blade, blend cream cheese, milk and seasoning & salad dressing mix until smooth. Cook pasta according to package directions; drain and combine with peas and tuna in a large skillet. Stir dressing mixture into pasta. Cook over low heat until mixture is hot.

Fettuccine with Chicken Breasts

Makes 8 servings

- 12 ounces uncooked fettuccine or egg noodles
- 1 cup Hidden Valley® Original Ranch® Dressing
- ⅓ cup Dijon mustard
- 8 boneless, skinless chicken breast halves, pounded thin
- ½ cup butter
- ⅓ cup dry white wine

Cook fettuccine according to package directions; drain. Preheat oven to 425°F. Stir together dressing and mustard; set aside. Pour fettuccine into oiled baking dish. Sauté chicken in butter in a large skillet until no longer pink in center. Transfer cooked chicken to the bed of fettuccine. Add wine to the skillet; cook until reduced to desired consistency. Drizzle over chicken. Pour the reserved dressing mixture over the chicken. Bake at 425°F. about 10 minutes, or until dressing forms a golden brown crust.

Turkey and Stuffing Bake

MAKES 4 TO 6 SERVINGS

- 1 jar (4½ ounces) sliced mushrooms
- ¼ cup butter or margarine
- ½ cup diced celery
- ½ cup chopped onion
- 1¼ cups Hidden Valley® Original Ranch® Dressing, divided
- ⅔ cup water
- 3 cups seasoned stuffing mix
- ⅓ cup sweetened dried cranberries
- 3 cups coarsely shredded cooked turkey (about 1 pound)

Drain mushrooms, reserving liquid; set aside. Melt butter over medium high heat in a large skillet. Add celery and onion; sauté for 4 minutes or until soft. Remove from heat and stir in ½ cup dressing, water and reserved mushroom liquid. Stir in stuffing mix and cranberries until thoroughly moistened. Combine turkey, mushrooms and remaining ¾ cup dressing in a separate bowl; spread evenly in a greased 8-inch baking dish. Top with stuffing mixture. Bake at 350°F. for 40 minutes or until bubbly and brown.

Turkey and Stuffing Bake

Spinach Lasagna Roll-Ups

MAKES 6 SERVINGS

- 8 ounces uncooked 2½-inch wide lasagna noodles (12 noodles)
- 1 package (8 ounces) cream cheese, softened
- 1 packet (1 ounce) Hidden Valley® Original Ranch® Seasoning & Salad Dressing Mix
- 1 package (10 ounces) frozen chopped spinach, thawed and squeezed dry
- 1 can (8 ounces) tomato sauce
- ¾ cup milk
- ¾ cup (3 ounces) shredded mozzarella cheese

Cook lasagna according to package directions. Rinse with cold water; drain well. Lay noodles on oiled baking sheets. Meanwhile, beat cream cheese and seasoning & salad dressing mix until smooth. Remove ½ cup cream cheese mixture and combine with spinach in a small mixing bowl. Spread about 2 tablespoons spinach mixture evenly on each noodle. Starting from narrow ends, roll up noodles and place, seam side down, in a 13×9-inch baking dish. Whisk tomato sauce and milk into remaining cream cheese mixture until smooth; pour sauce evenly over roll-ups. Cover with foil. Bake at 325°F. for 25 minutes. Sprinkle roll-ups with mozzarella cheese, cover loosely and continue baking 10 minutes longer or until hot and bubbly.

Spinach Lasagna Roll-Ups

Outrageous Ranch Tacos

Makes 4 servings

1 pound lean ground beef
3 cups shredded lettuce
½ cup Hidden Valley® Original Ranch® Dressing
8 large taco shells, heated
½ cup (2 ounces) shredded Cheddar cheese
1 medium tomato, diced (optional)

Brown beef in a large skillet, crumbling into small pieces; drain. Toss lettuce with dressing. Fill each taco shell with about ¼ cup beef, an eighth of lettuce mixture and 1 tablespoon cheese. Top with tomato, if desired.

Chicken Caesar Primavera

Makes 4 servings

6 ounces uncooked spiral egg noodles or rotini
2 cups shredded or cubed cooked chicken
2 cups cooked mixed vegetables, such as broccoli, cauliflower and peppers
1 cup Hidden Valley® Caesar with Crushed Garlic
½ cup chicken broth
½ cup grated Parmesan cheese

Cook pasta according to package directions. Drain and combine with chicken, vegetables, dressing and broth in a large saucepan. Heat thoroughly. Sprinkle with cheese before serving.

Original Ranch® Beef and Noodle Skillet

Makes 4 servings

- 8 ounces uncooked wide egg noodles
- 1 pound lean ground beef, cooked and drained
- 1 container (8 ounces) sour cream (1 cup)
- ¾ cup milk
- 1 jar (4½ ounces) sliced mushrooms, drained
- 1 packet (1 ounce) Hidden Valley® Original Ranch® Seasoning & Salad Dressing Mix
- ½ cup grated Parmesan cheese
- Sliced green onions (optional)

Cook noodles according to package directions. Drain and combine with ground beef, sour cream, milk, mushrooms and seasoning & salad dressing mix. Cook and stir until thoroughly heated. Sprinkle with cheese. Garnish with onions, if desired.

Chicken Caesar Tetrazzini

MAKES 4 SERVINGS

- 8 ounces uncooked spaghetti
- 2 cups shredded or cubed cooked chicken
- 1 cup chicken broth
- 1 cup Hidden Valley® Caesar with Crushed Garlic
- 1 jar (4½ ounces) sliced mushrooms, drained
- ½ cup grated Parmesan cheese
- 2 tablespoons dry bread crumbs

Cook spaghetti according to package directions. Drain and combine with chicken, broth, dressing and mushrooms in a large mixing bowl. Place mixture in a 2-quart casserole. Mix together cheese and bread crumbs; sprinkle over spaghetti mixture. Bake at 350°F. for 25 minutes or until casserole is hot and bubbly.

Chicken Caesar Tetrazzini

Ranch Baked Quesadillas

Makes 4 servings

- 1 cup shredded cooked chicken
- 1 cup (4 ounces) shredded Monterey Jack cheese
- ½ cup Hidden Valley® Original Ranch® Dressing
- ¼ cup diced green chiles, rinsed and drained
- 4 (9-inch) flour tortillas, heated
- Salsa and guacamole (optional)

Combine chicken, cheese, dressing and chiles in a medium bowl. Place about ½ cup chicken mixture on each tortilla; fold in half. Place quesadillas on a baking sheet. Bake at 350°F. for 15 minutes or until cheese is melted. Cut into thirds, if desired. Serve with salsa and guacamole, if desired.

Ranch Baked Quesadillas

Spinach Tortellini with Roasted Red Peppers

MAKES 4 TO 6 SERVINGS

- 2 packages (9 ounces *each*) refrigerated spinach tortellini
- 1 jar (7 ounces) roasted red peppers, rinsed and drained
- 2 tablespoons butter or olive oil
- 4 cloves garlic, minced
- ¼ cup chopped fresh basil *or* 2 teaspoons dried basil, crushed
- ½ cup chopped walnuts or pine nuts, toasted
- 1 cup Hidden Valley® Original Ranch® Dressing
- Fresh basil leaves (optional)

Cook tortellini according to package directions; drain and set aside. Slice red peppers into strips; set aside. Melt butter in medium saucepan; add garlic and sauté for about 2 minutes. Stir in tortellini, red pepper strips, basil and walnuts. Stir in dressing until mixture is creamy and tortellini are coated. Garnish with basil leaves, if desired.

Spinach Tortellini with Roasted Red Peppers

SATISFYING SALADS

Chopstick Chicken Salad

MAKES 4 TO 6 SERVINGS

- 1 cup Hidden Valley® Original Ranch® Dressing
- 1 tablespoon soy sauce
- 8 cups torn lettuce
- 2 cups shredded cooked chicken
- 1 cup chopped green onions
- 1 can (8 ounces) sliced water chestnuts, rinsed and drained
- ½ cup sliced almonds, toasted

Whisk together dressing and soy sauce in a small bowl. Combine lettuce, chicken, green onions and water chestnuts in a large salad bowl; toss with dressing mixture. Top with almonds just before serving.

Outrageous Mexican Chicken Salad

Makes 4 to 6 servings

- 6 cups shredded lettuce
- 1 bag (9 ounces) tortilla chips, crushed (about 3 cups)
- 2 cups cubed cooked chicken
- 1 can (15½ ounces) kidney beans, rinsed and drained
- 1½ cups Hidden Valley® Original Ranch® Dressing
- ½ cup (2 ounces) shredded Cheddar cheese
- Tomatoes and olives, for garnish

Combine lettuce, chips, chicken, beans, dressing and cheese in a large bowl. Garnish with tomatoes and olives.

Crunchy Pea Salad

MAKES 6 TO 8 SERVINGS

- 1 package (10 ounces) frozen petite peas *or* 2 cups fresh peas
- 1 cup diced celery
- 1 cup chopped cauliflower
- 1 cup chopped cashew nuts
- 1/4 cup diced green onions
- 1/4 cup crisp-cooked, crumbled bacon*
- 2 tablespoons chopped pimientos
- 3/4 cup Hidden Valley® Original Ranch® Dressing
- 1/4 cup sour cream
- 1/2 teaspoon Dijon mustard

**Bacon pieces may be used.*

Rinse frozen peas in hot water (or steam fresh peas); drain. Combine peas, celery, cauliflower, cashew nuts, onions, bacon and pimientos in a large bowl. Whisk together dressing, sour cream and mustard in a small bowl; pour over salad mixture. Toss gently. Chill.

Mediterranean Orzo Salad

MAKES 4 TO 6 SERVINGS

SALAD

- 1 cup orzo pasta
- 1 cup diced red bell pepper
- ½ cup crumbled feta cheese
- 1 can (2¼ ounces) sliced ripe olives, rinsed and drained
- ¼ cup chopped fresh basil *or* ½ teaspoon dried basil
- Fresh basil leaves or parsley sprigs, for garnish (optional)

DRESSING

- 1 packet (1 ounce) Hidden Valley® Original Ranch® Seasoning & Salad Dressing Mix
- 3 tablespoons olive oil
- 3 tablespoons red wine vinegar
- 1 teaspoon sugar

Cook orzo according to package directions, omitting salt. Rinse with cold water and drain well. Mix orzo, bell pepper, cheese, olives and chopped fresh basil in a large bowl. (If using dried basil, add to dressing.) Whisk together seasoning & salad dressing mix, oil, vinegar and sugar. Stir dressing into orzo mixture. Cover and refrigerate at least 2 hours. Garnish with basil leaves before serving, if desired.

Mediterranean Orzo Salad

Ranch Picnic Potato Salad

MAKES 8 SERVINGS

- 6 medium potatoes (about 3½ pounds), cooked, peeled and sliced
- ½ cup chopped celery
- ¼ cup sliced green onions
- 2 tablespoons chopped parsley
- 1 teaspoon salt
- ⅛ teaspoon black pepper
- 1 cup Hidden Valley® Original Ranch® Dressing
- 1 tablespoon Dijon mustard
- 2 hard-cooked eggs, finely chopped
- Paprika
- Lettuce (optional)

Combine potatoes, celery, onions, parsley, salt and pepper in a large bowl. Stir together dressing and mustard in a small bowl; pour over potato mixture and toss lightly. Cover and refrigerate several hours. Sprinkle with eggs and paprika. Serve in a lettuce-lined bowl, if desired.

Ranch Picnic Potato Salad

Hidden Valley® BBQ Ranch™ Chicken Salad

Makes 4 to 6 servings

½ cup Hidden Valley® BBQ Ranch™ Dressing
2 cups cubed cooked chicken
1 can (15 ounces) black beans, rinsed and drained
1 cup (11 ounces) corn, drained
1 cup diced tomato
Chopped lettuce*
1 red bell pepper, diced, as garnish

In a medium bowl, gently combine all ingredients. Serve chilled over chopped lettuce and garnish with diced red bell pepper.

***Pasta Variation:** Eliminate lettuce. Gently toss 3 cups cooked rotelle or wagon wheel pasta with other salad ingredients.

Bacon Vinaigrette Dressing

MAKES ABOUT 3/4 CUP

1 packet (1 ounce) Hidden Valley® Original Ranch® Seasoning & Salad Dressing Mix
1/4 cup vegetable oil
1/4 cup water
2 tablespoons cider vinegar
2 tablespoons crisp-cooked, crumbled bacon*
1 tablespoon light brown sugar

**Bacon pieces may be used.*

Whisk together seasoning & salad dressing mix, oil, water, vinegar, bacon and brown sugar. Serve over your favorite salad blend.

SERVING SUGGESTION: For a tasty spinach salad, toss dressing with torn spinach, sliced fresh mushrooms, quartered cherry tomatoes and croutons.

Ranch Tuna Stuffed Tomatoes

MAKES 4 SERVINGS

- 1 can (6 ounces) solid white tuna, drained
- 1 can (8 ounces) kidney beans, rinsed and drained
- 1 can (8 ounces) corn, drained
- 1 cup (4 ounces) shredded mild Cheddar cheese
- ⅔ cup Hidden Valley® Original Ranch® Dressing
- ¼ cup chopped green onions
- 4 large fresh tomatoes (at least 8 ounces each)

Flake tuna and combine with beans, corn, cheese, dressing and onions in a medium bowl. Cover and chill 1 hour. Just before serving, core each tomato and carefully scoop out center to within ¼ inch of edge, forming a bowl; discard flesh and seeds. Drain tomatoes upside down on paper towels. Cut each tomato into 5 or 6 wedges, leaving the bottom intact. Gently open each tomato to support the salad. Arrange tuna mixture on top of the tomatoes.

Ranch Tuna Stuffed Tomato

Thai Beef Salad

MAKES 4 SERVINGS

- ¾ cup mayonnaise
- ¾ cup unsweetened coconut milk
- 1 packet (1 ounce) Hidden Valley® Original Ranch® Seasoning & Salad Dressing Mix
- 2 tablespoons lime juice
- 1 pound thinly sliced roast beef
- 1 English cucumber, thinly sliced
- 1 cup sliced bamboo shoots
- ¼ cup cilantro leaves
- ¼ cup coarsely chopped peanuts

Combine mayonnaise, coconut milk, seasoning & salad dressing mix and lime juice in a small bowl; chill 30 minutes. Arrange beef, cucumber, bamboo shoots and cilantro on a large platter. Pour dressing in a thin stream over salad. Sprinkle with peanuts.

Thai Beef Salad

Napa Valley Chicken Salad

Makes 4 servings

2 cups diced cooked chicken
1 cup seedless red grapes, halved
1 cup diced celery
½ cup chopped toasted pecans
¼ cup thinly sliced green onions
½ cup Hidden Valley® Original Ranch® Dressing
1 teaspoon Dijon mustard

Combine chicken, grapes, celery, pecans and onions in a medium bowl. Stir together dressing and mustard; toss with salad. Cover and refrigerate for 2 hours.

Salinas Ranch Dressing

Makes 2 cups

2 cups Hidden Valley® Original Ranch® Dressing
½ cup finely chopped drained marinated artichoke hearts
¼ cup grated Parmesan cheese

Stir together dressing, artichoke hearts and cheese. Chill.

Serving Suggestion: Serve dressing over mixed salad greens, cold cooked chicken or cold poached fish.

Napa Valley Chicken Salad

Pasta Primavera Salad

MAKES 4 TO 6 SERVINGS

- 12 ounces uncooked spiral egg noodles or rotini pasta
- 3 tablespoons olive oil
- 1 cup broccoli florets, steamed and cooled
- 1 large red or green bell pepper, cut into small chunks
- 2 medium zucchini, cut into ¼-inch slices
- ½ cup cherry tomato halves
- ⅓ cup sliced radishes
- 3 green onions, chopped
- 1 cup Hidden Valley® Original Ranch® Dressing

Cook pasta according to package directions. Rinse with cold water and drain well. Toss pasta with oil in a large bowl. Add broccoli, bell peppers, zucchini, tomatoes, radishes and green onions; toss again. Add dressing and toss to coat. Cover and refrigerate 2 hours. Just before serving, add more dressing, if desired.

Florentine Salad

MAKES 4 TO 6 SERVINGS

- 4 cups torn spinach leaves
- 4 cups torn romaine lettuce leaves
- 1 cup sliced fresh mushrooms
- ½ cup coarsely chopped red onion
- ¼ cup crisp-cooked, crumbled bacon*
- ½ cup Hidden Valley® Original Ranch® Dressing
- 1 cup mandarin oranges, drained

**Bacon pieces may be used.*

Wash spinach and lettuce; blot dry. Combine with mushrooms, onion and bacon in a large salad bowl. Toss with dressing. Top with orange segments.

SAVORY SIDES

Original Ranch® Roasted Potatoes

MAKES 4 TO 6 SERVINGS

- 2 pounds small red potatoes, quartered
- ¼ cup vegetable oil
- 1 packet (1 ounce) Hidden Valley® Original Ranch® Seasoning & Salad Dressing Mix

Place potatoes in a gallon-size Glad® Zipper Storage Bag. Pour oil over potatoes. Seal bag and toss to coat. Add seasoning & salad dressing mix; seal bag and toss again until coated. Bake in ungreased baking pan at 450°F. for 30 to 35 minutes or until potatoes are brown and crisp.

Sweet & Tangy Marinated Vegetables

Makes 8 servings

- 8 cups mixed fresh vegetables, such as broccoli, cauliflower, zucchini, carrots and red bell peppers, cut into 1 to 1½-inch pieces
- ⅓ cup distilled white vinegar
- ¼ cup sugar
- ¼ cup water
- 1 packet (1 ounce) Hidden Valley® Original Ranch® Seasoning & Salad Dressing Mix

Place vegetables in a gallon size Glad® Zipper Storage Bag. Whisk together vinegar, sugar, water and seasoning & salad dressing mix until sugar dissolves; pour over vegetables. Seal bag and shake to coat. Refrigerate 4 hours or overnight, turning bag occasionally.

NOTE: Vegetables will keep up to 3 days in refrigerator.

Hidden Valley® Glazed Baby Carrots

Makes 4 to 6 servings

- ¼ cup butter
- ¼ cup packed light brown sugar
- 1 package (16 ounces) ready-to-eat baby carrots, cooked
- 1 packet (1 ounce) Hidden Valley® Original Ranch® Seasoning & Salad Dressing Mix

Melt butter and sugar in a large skillet. Add carrots and seasoning & salad dressing mix; stir well. Cook over medium heat until carrots are tender and glazed, about 5 minutes, stirring frequently.

Southwestern Rice

MAKES 6 SERVINGS

- 1 cup uncooked converted rice
- 1 can (15 ounces) black beans, rinsed and drained
- 1 can (8 ounces) corn, drained
- 1 packet (1 ounce) Hidden Valley® Original Ranch® Seasoning & Salad Dressing Mix
- ¾ cup (3 ounces) diced Monterey Jack cheese
- ½ cup seeded, diced tomato
- ¼ cup sliced green onions

Cook rice according to package directions, omitting salt. During last five minutes of cooking time, quickly uncover and add beans and corn; cover immediately. When rice is done, remove saucepan from heat; add seasoning & salad dressing mix and stir. Let stand 5 minutes. Stir in cheese, tomato and onions. Serve immediately.

Southwestern Rice

Ranch Pilaf

MAKES 4 TO 6 SERVINGS

- 2 tablespoons butter
- 1 cup uncooked long grain rice
- ½ cup finely chopped red onion
- 1¾ cups chicken broth
- ½ cup shredded carrot
- 1 packet (1 ounce) Hidden Valley® Original Ranch® Seasoning & Salad Dressing Mix
- ¼ cup slivered almonds, toasted

Melt butter in large skillet over medium-high heat. Add rice and onion; sauté about 6 minutes or until golden. Stir in broth, carrot and seasoning & salad dressing mix; bring to boil. Transfer to a 2-quart baking dish; cover and bake at 350°F. for 30 minutes. Before serving, fluff rice with fork and sprinkle with almonds.

NOTE: For stove-top method, increase chicken broth to 2¼ cups. Reduce heat; simmer, covered, over low heat for 20 minutes or until rice is tender. Fluff rice with fork; transfer from skillet to serving bowl and sprinkle with almonds.

Broiled Ranch Mushrooms

Makes 4 to 6 servings

- 1 pound medium mushrooms
- 1 packet (1 ounce) Hidden Valley® Original Ranch® Seasoning & Salad Dressing Mix
- ¼ cup vegetable oil
- ¼ cup water
- 1 tablespoon balsamic vinegar

Place mushrooms in a gallon-size Glad® Zipper Storage Bag. Whisk together seasoning & salad dressing mix, oil, water and vinegar. Pour over mushrooms; seal bag and marinate in refrigerator for 30 minutes, turning occasionally. Place mushrooms on a broiling rack. Broil 4 inches from heat for about 8 minutes or until tender.

Creamy Broccoli and Cheese

MAKES 4 SERVINGS

1 package (8 ounces) cream cheese, softened
¾ cup milk
1 packet (1 ounce) Hidden Valley® Original Ranch® Seasoning & Salad Dressing Mix
1 pound fresh broccoli, cooked and drained
½ cup (2 ounces) shredded sharp Cheddar cheese

In a food processor fitted with a metal blade, blend cream cheese, milk and seasoning & salad dressing mix until smooth. Pour over broccoli in a 9-inch baking dish; stir well. Top with cheese. Bake at 350°F. for 25 minutes or until cheese is melted.

Original Ranch® Mashed Potatoes

MAKES 4 SERVINGS

4 cups hot unsalted mashed potatoes (with or without skins)
1 packet (1 ounce) Hidden Valley® Original Ranch® Seasoning & Salad Dressing Mix
Butter or margarine (optional)

Combine potatoes and seasoning & salad dressing mix; stir well. Serve with butter or margarine, if desired.

Ranch Bacon Potato Topper

MAKES 1½ CUPS POTATO TOPPER

- 1 package (8 ounces) cream cheese, softened
- ¾ cup Hidden Valley® Original Ranch® Dressing
- ¼ cup sour cream
- 2 teaspoons crisp-cooked, crumbled bacon*
- 2 teaspoons minced green onion
- 6 hot medium baked potatoes

**Bacon pieces may be used.*

In a food processor fitted with a metal blade, blend together cream cheese, dressing and sour cream. Add bacon and onion; pulse 3 to 4 times. Serve over baked potatoes.

Original Ranch® & Cheddar Bread

MAKES 16 PIECES

- 1 cup Hidden Valley® Original Ranch® Dressing
- 2 cups (8 ounces) shredded sharp Cheddar cheese
- 1 whole loaf (1 pound) French bread (not sour dough)

Stir together dressing and cheese. Cut bread in half lengthwise. Place on a broiler pan and spread dressing mixture evenly over cut side of each half. Broil until lightly brown. Cut each half into 8 pieces.

Burger Topper

MAKES 1 CUP TOPPER

- ¾ cup Hidden Valley® Original Ranch® Dressing
- ¼ cup thinly sliced green onions
- 2 tablespoons KC Masterpiece® Barbecue Sauce

Stir together dressing, onions and barbecue sauce. Serve 1 to 2 tablespoons mixture on a hamburger or turkey burger.

Original Ranch® & Cheddar Bread

SENSATIONAL SANDWICHES

Hidden Valley® Wraps

MAKES 4 SERVINGS

1 cup Hidden Valley® Original Ranch® Dressing
1 package (8 ounces) cream cheese, softened
10 ounces sliced turkey breast
10 ounces Monterey Jack cheese slices
2 large avocados, peeled and thinly sliced
2 medium tomatoes, thinly sliced
Shredded lettuce
4 (12-inch) flour tortillas, warmed

Beat together dressing and cream cheese. Evenly layer half the turkey, Monterey Jack cheese, dressing mixture, avocados, tomatoes and lettuce among tortillas, leaving a 1-inch border around edges. Repeat layering with remaining ingredients. Fold right and left edges of tortillas into centers over the filling. Fold the bottom edge toward the center and roll firmly until completely wrapped. Place seam side down and cut in half diagonally.

Open-Faced Italian Focaccia Sandwich

Makes 4 servings

- 2 cups shredded cooked chicken
- ½ cup Hidden Valley® Original Ranch® Dressing
- ¼ cup diagonally sliced green onions
- 1 piece focaccia bread, about ¾-inch thick, 10×7-inches
- 2 medium tomatoes, thinly sliced
- 4 cheese slices, such as provolone, Cheddar or Swiss
- 2 tablespoons grated Parmesan cheese (optional)

Stir together chicken, dressing and onions in a small mixing bowl. Arrange chicken mixture evenly on top of focaccia. Top with layer of tomatoes and cheese slices. Sprinkle with Parmesan cheese, if desired. Broil 2 minutes or until cheese is melted and bubbly.

Note: Purchase rotisserie chicken at your favorite store to add great taste and save preparation time.

Open-Faced Italian Focaccia Sandwich

Ham Salad Bread Bowls

MAKES 4 SERVINGS (OR 3 CUPS SALAD)

- 3/4 pound thick sliced deli ham
- 2/3 cup shredded Swiss cheese
- 1/2 cup Hidden Valley® Original Ranch® Dressing
- 1/4 cup chopped green onions
- 1/4 cup finely chopped sweet gherkin or dill pickles
- 4 whole Kaiser rolls (4-inch diameter)

Finely dice ham to make about 2 1/3 cups; combine with cheese, dressing, onions and pickles in a medium mixing bowl. Cut a thin slice off the top of each roll. Scoop out center to within 1/4 inch from edge, forming a bowl. Stuff ham salad gently into bread bowls.

Ham Salad Bread Bowl

INDEX